SPORTS JOURNALISM

DIANE DAKERS

Crabtree Publishing Company
www.crabtreebooks.com

Author: Diane Dakers

Series research and development: Janine Deschenes, Reagan Miller

Editorial director: Kathy Middleton

Editor: Janine Deschenes

Proofreaders: Wendy Scavuzzo, Melissa Boyce

Design and photo research: Katherine Berti

Print and production coordinator: Katherine Berti

Images:

Getty Images
Bruce Kluckhohn: p. 30
Jeff Kowalsky: p. 38
Rena Laverty: p. 40
interactives.indystar.com
Screen Shot 2018-07-13 at 10.05.51 AM: p. 36
Keystone Press
Minneapolis Star Tribune/ ZUMA: p. 26
ZUMAPRESS.com: front cover (center left), p. 25 (top)
Shutterstock
Andrew Makedonski: p. 13 (bottom left)
Bjoern Wylezich: front cover (newspapers)
Denis Linine: p. 21
imagestockdesign: p. 4 (right)
Jefferson Bernardes: p. 14 (bottom right)
John De La Bastide: front cover (top left, front), p. 20 (bottom right)
JStone: front cover (bottom left), p. 41
kojoku: p. 14 (bottom left)
Leonard Zhukovsky: p. 35 (bottom), 24 (right)
mbond77: p. 5 (stadium, back)
Natursports: p. 11
Oleksandr Osipov: p. 17
Patrick Tuohy: front cover (center left)
Rob Marmion: p. 25 (bottom)
Rob Wilson: p. 5 (FIFA World Cup, front)
Sergei Butorin: p. 24 (bottom left)
Ugis Riba: front cover (top left, back)
Valery Bocman: P. 13 (bottom right)
Vlad1988: p. 15 (top)
XanderSt: p. 16 (bottom left, inset)
Wikimedia Commons
Boston University Center for the Study of Traumatic Encephalopathy: p. 32
José Cruz: p. 23 (top left)
www.playthegame.org
Screen Shot 2018-07-12 at 11.50.31 AM: p. 23 (bottom right)
All other images by Shutterstock

Library and Archives Canada Cataloguing in Publication

Dakers, Diane, author
Sports journalism / Diane Dakers.

(Investigative journalism that inspired change)
Includes bibliographical references and index.
Issued in print and electronic formats.
ISBN 978-0-7787-5352-0 (hardcover).--
ISBN 978-0-7787-5365-0 (softcover).--
ISBN 978-1-4271-2199-8 (HTML)

1. Sports journalism--Juvenile literature. 2. Sports journalism--Case studies--Juvenile literature. 3. Sports--Press coverage--Juvenile literature. 4. Mass media and sports--Juvenile literature. I. Title.

PN4784.S6D35 2018   j070.4'49796   C2018-905449-2
C2018-905450-6

Library of Congress Cataloging-in-Publication Data

Names: Dakers, Diane, author.
Title: Sports journalism / Diane Dakers.
Description: New York : Crabtree Publishing Company, 2018. | Series: Investigative journalism that inspired change | Includes bibliographical references and index.
Identifiers: LCCN 2018043622 (print) | LCCN 2018049815 (ebook) | ISBN 9781427121998 (Electronic) | ISBN 9780778753520 (hardcover) | ISBN 9780778753650 (pbk.)
Subjects: LCSH: Sports journalism--Juvenile literature.
Classification: LCC PN4784.S6 (ebook) | LCC PN4784.S6 D25 2018 (print) | DDC 070.4/49796--dc23
LC record available at https://lccn.loc.gov/2018043622

Crabtree Publishing Company

www.crabtreebooks.com   1-800-387-7650

Printed in the U.S.A./122018/CG20181005

Published in Canada
Crabtree Publishing
616 Welland Ave.
St. Catharines, Ontario
L2M 5V6

Published in the United States
Crabtree Publishing
PMB 59051
350 Fifth Avenue, 59th Floor
New York, New York 10118

Published in the United Kingdom
Crabtree Publishing
Maritime House
Basin Road North, Hove
BN41 1WR

Published in Australia
Crabtree Publishing
3 Charles Street
Coburg North
VIC 3058

CONTENTS

INVESTIGATING SPORTS

Investigative journalists are reporters who write in-depth, detailed stories about certain issues and topics. They can report on sports topics, but are different from ***conventional*** *sports reporters who write the facts about games, teams, and players.*

Soccer—or football, as it's called in most countries—is the most popular sport in the world. The World Cup final, for example, is the most-watched sporting event in the world.

The organization that oversees the international soccer community is the *Fédération Internationale de Football Association* (FIFA). This group also stages major international tournaments, including the World Cup—and it rakes in the dough. For example, FIFA earned billions from the 2018 World Cup in Russia. But where does all that money go?

That's what British investigative journalist Andrew Jennings asked himself in 2002. He spent the next 13 years answering that question. What he discovered was something the football community—and his fellow sports journalists—didn't want to know about.

By reading thousands of private FIFA documents and interviewing dozens of people, Andrew learned the organization was full of **corrupt** executives, or business leaders. They accepted **bribes**, paid themselves hundreds of thousands of dollars in "bonuses," sold event tickets illegally, and **rigged** votes to determine which countries hosted World Cup events.

In short, these executives got rich using money that should have been used to support teams, players, and football events around the world.

> This is a culture, a system that has cheated every fan. The sport has been cheated. Imagine all those millions that are pouring into football being used in a proper manner. [...] A properly run **administrative body** would have made more money from the game and **distributed** it so much better.

Andrew Jennings, 2015

In 2006, Andrew wrote his first stories and his first book on the corruption at FIFA. Over the next eight years, he produced three half-hour TV segments and wrote another book on the subject.

However, at first the story made no waves in the sporting world. Other sports journalists wanted nothing to do with the story—or with Andrew—because they knew it would harm their professional relationship with FIFA. And FIFA certainly didn't want fans to know what was going on behind closed doors. In fact, many people tried to shut down Andrew's investigation to keep the story quiet. He was banned from FIFA events and received threats from those who objected to his work. FIFA executives harassed him. Even his fellow sports reporters **shunned** him. Still, this dedicated investigative journalist didn't give up. In a 2016 interview, Andrew said he didn't care how long it took him to get the full FIFA story. He trusted that, "eventually, it would break."

Indeed, the story of FIFA corruption finally broke wide open in 2015. In June of that year, police in the United States and Switzerland arrested 14 FIFA executives. The men were charged with criminal activities involving more than $200 million in bribes.

At last, the world knew Andrew had been right about the organization all along. They could no longer ignore the story he'd been working to tell since 2002.

COMMITMENT, DETERMINATION, AND DEDICATION TO THE TRUTH

Andrew Jennings's drive to expose wrongdoing is what fueled his 13-year investigation. "It goes back to what your mother told you as a kid: 'If you do bad things then you will get caught.' I want to show that is true," he said.

This commitment to revealing truths others want hidden is a trait common to all investigative journalists. Other traits they have in common include patience, because projects can take years; courage, because others may try to stop them from exposing the truth; and creativity, because they have to come up with new ways to find hidden information.

An investigative journalism project usually starts with a question. Andrew, for example, wondered what happened to all the money FIFA earned. A journalist's initial question might stem from simple curiosity, witnessing wrongdoing, or overhearing a private conversation. Sometimes, members of the public "leak," or secretly provide, documents or other information that lead journalists to investigate. Journalists might also read other news stories that raise questions in their minds.

Once an investigative journalist has a story idea, he or she comes up with a plan to research the subject. A plan might involve requesting and reviewing stacks of **legal** or **public documents**, interviewing a variety of people, and analyzing data. Journalists often travel to speak with witnesses and experts, allowing them to observe the effects of a story in person.

A DEFINITION AND AN EXPLANATION

The **United Nations** defines investigative journalism as "the unveiling of matters that are **concealed** either deliberately by someone in a position of power, or accidentally, behind a **chaotic** mass of facts and circumstances—and the analysis and exposure of all relevant facts to the public."

That means investigative journalists uncover hidden stories, research them, and report them to the public. These stories are sometimes purposely hidden. Other times, they are buried so deep in documents, data, and details that nobody has dug them up yet.

The research process can take months or years to complete. Every detail has to be double-checked and confirmed by a variety of **sources**. That's because an investigative journalism story cannot be released to the public without absolute proof that it is true. If a story contains errors, the journalist and media outlet could suffer legal and professional penalties. A reporter could be sued, for example, for publishing incorrect information that damages a person's, or a business's, reputation. In addition, reporters who repeatedly get their facts wrong could lose the trust and respect of their colleagues and communities.

Others involved in a story, could also be hurt by incorrect information. Therefore, journalists must also follow laws and ethical standards to protect people's privacy and reputations.

Sources can be such things as people who are knowledgeable about the subject, government documents, and legal records.

ROLES AND RESPONSIBILITIES

Journalists must follow certain laws as they research and write their stories. These laws cover such things as when and where a reporter can take photos or use a recording device. Other laws prevent reporters from making false statements that might damage someone's reputation. **Copyright laws** make sure reporters have permission to use material they want to publish.

In addition to laws are codes of **ethics** journalists follow. These are guidelines that describe appropriate and inappropriate behavior for journalists. Different media organizations have different codes of ethics, but most require their reporters to be truthful, accurate, fair, and objective in their work.

Because so much work is involved in gathering, compiling, reviewing, and fact-checking a story's details, investigative journalism projects usually involve many people, such as reporters, **editors**, and **data analysts**. The number of people and amount of time involved in investigative journalism are two of the things that set it apart from conventional, or daily, journalism.

Another difference is that conventional journalism often focuses on reporting information provided by others. Police and fire departments, politicians, and businesses, for example, often give daily news reporters information to pass on to the public.

Investigative journalists look beyond such material. They often seek out the kinds of information that governments and others don't want the public to know.

The goal of investigative journalism is to uncover wrongdoing, crime, or other issues that have an impact on humanity—and to share the truth with members of the public.

Investigative journalists are not activists. They don't actively protest or fight for change—but their work often encourages others to take action, or at least to make well-informed decisions.

The work of investigative journalists can make a global impact. Their stories encourage people around the world to question the information they receive, speak out against wrongdoing, and demand the truth.

INVESTIGATIVE OR CONVENTIONAL?

Different people and organizations define investigative journalism in different ways. However, most agree that it differs from conventional reporting in a number of areas:

INVESTIGATIVE JOURNALISM

- Reporter is **proactive** in looking for original stories on which to report
- Projects are long-term and require in-depth research
- Goal of reporters is to question
- Projects expose issues surrounded in secrecy or silence
- Work often leads to social change

CONVENTIONAL JOURNALISM

- Reporter reacts to information provided by sources such as police, governments, or businesses
- Projects are short-term
- Goal of reporters is to inform about facts as they are
- Presents news, events, and happenings of the day

A TEAM EFFORT

Investigative journalism is rarely a solo activity. Today, most investigative journalism projects are **multimedia** presentations that a variety of people work to create.

First, there are reporters. They might be newspaper, or print, journalists who conduct interviews, gather facts, and write a story. Photographers almost always accompany reporters to take pictures that will illustrate the story.

In the case of television or video projects, videographers accompany reporters. These are people who record every aspect of a particular story—including interviews, events, and story locations.

Because most investigative journalism projects end up online, most of them include all of these elements—words, photos, and video. Some also include audio, or sound, segments.

Graphic designers are also involved in the final product. They add such things as maps, charts, and infographics. Fact-checkers are people who double-check every detail in a project.

Before any story is presented to the public, editors read or view it to make sure it makes sense and that all of the relevant information is included. Then, at least one more person checks it for typos, missing elements, or technical glitches.

> There is passion [for the story], but there is also the hard work of sifting through e-mails, tallying figures and exchanging information with **contacts** and other journalists. [...] We are only reporters. Our job is to discover the documents, amass the evidence and get the sources. That is hard work.

Investigative journalist Andrew Jennings, 2015

REPORTING ON SPORTING

Almost any topic can be the subject of an investigative journalism project, but investigative sports journalism is a relatively new field. Andrew Jennings is considered one of the pioneers of this type of investigative reporting. In the late-1990s, he produced a series of stories about wrongdoing among Olympic officials. The series, which revealed that officials had accepted bribes to ensure certain cities hosted the Olympics or to make sure certain athletes won their competitions, is considered one of the first examples of investigative sports reporting.

Since then, investigative journalists have tackled such sporting subjects as drug use and abuse among athletes, academic cheating by college athletes, and the high death rate of racehorses.

This book focuses on three specific sports investigations—a project about the life, death, and brain damage of a professional hockey player; a piece about the long-term abuse of young American gymnasts; and Andrew Jennings's FIFA story.

The reporter who covered the hockey player's life relied on interviews, private papers, and game footage to piece together his story. The team of journalists who discovered child abuse in the gymnastics world traveled across America for two years interviewing affected girls and their families. They also reviewed thousands of pages of police and **court** records. And after piecing together documents and interviews to expose FIFA's corruption, Andrew Jennings steadfastly refused to let the story die, no matter how hard people tried to stop him from telling it.

Like most investigative projects, these ones started with a question, an unexpected discovery, or a sense that something wasn't right. The reporters' passion, curiosity, and quest for truth then took over—driving them to expose wrongdoings that affected the lives of athletes and fans around the world.

THE DIRTY GAME

WHO	FIFA executives
WHAT	Stole millions of dollars
WHEN	Approximately 1990 to 2015
WHERE	Around the world
WHY	Greed
HOW	Accepted bribes, paid themselves millions of dollars, rigged voting systems

For decades, British **independent journalist** Andrew Jennings covered stories about international organized crime. Organized crime is illegal activity planned and carried out by powerful people around the world.

Andrew wrote about such things as the international drug trade, dishonest police officers, and illegal weapons sales. In the 1990s, a colleague suggested he look into the **International Olympic Committee**—so Andrew turned his attention to sports.

In a 10-year investigation, he discovered that a number of Olympic executives were dishonest. Some took bribes to make sure certain athletes won specific competitions. Others stole money that was supposed to go to sports organizations. Some rigged votes to make sure particular cities won the right to host the Olympics. Overall, Andrew showed that the Olympic executives had created an international "ring" of organized crime. He wrote three books on the subject, then turned his focus to FIFA.

ORGANIZED CRIME

The United Nations defines organized crime as a crime committed by a group of people who work together. Their goal is to get money or receive other benefits. The people involved are usually in positions of power.

Any kind of journalist can investigate and report on organized crime. Andrew has spent much of his career focusing on organized crime in sports.

Often, the more knowledgeable an investigative journalist becomes about a particular subject, the more easily he or she recognizes related news stories. Andrew, for example, had years of experience researching organized crime. The Olympics then introduced him to organized crime in international sports. That, in turn, led him to question international football.

Andrew knew that football, or soccer, was even more popular, and earned more money, than the Olympics.

He wondered who controlled FIFA, and how they were using the billions of dollars that came into the organization. Drawing on his experience researching organized crime, Andrew had a hunch that something was wrong at FIFA.

In 2002, he tested his theory. Like all investigative journalists, Andrew started with clear questions: "Who were these guys in charge of FIFA? Where did all that money go?" He knew he would need to take risks to find that information.

From his knowledge of organized crime, Andrew knew that the people at the top—those who were organizing and benefiting from crime—would not provide the answers he needed. Instead, he knew there would be others in the organization who were aware of what was going on and would want to do the right thing. Those were the people he wanted to reach.

With that in mind, Andrew **ambushed** FIFA president Sepp Blatter at a **press conference** in 2002. He grabbed the microphone and asked, "***Herr*** Blatter, have you ever taken a bribe?"

Investigative journalists often take risks in their work to get the information they need. Andrew knew that, after that moment, he would be kicked out of the press conference. He knew he would never be allowed at FIFA games or events again. He knew his fellow sports journalists would avoid him.

But Andrew also knew that other FIFA employees were at the press conference. He wanted them to hear his question. His goal was to let those employees know that he suspected something was wrong at FIFA, and that they could come to him with information.

Of course, Sepp Blatter denied ever taking a bribe. He threatened to sue Andrew for spreading false information about him, but never followed through on the threat.

However, Andrew's plan worked. Six weeks after the press conference, a senior FIFA employee secretly gave Andrew a stack of documents. This employee also connected Andrew with other senior officials who had access to secret documents—and were willing to share them with the journalist. What followed were mounds of paperwork delivered to the reporter by many FIFA employees. Thirteen years later, Andrew said employees were still bringing him secret FIFA papers.

Sepp Blatter was FIFA president from 1998 until 2015, when he ***resigned****.*

Sports journalists need to have good relationships with sports organizations, such as FIFA, to get information for stories. Andrew gave up his relationship with FIFA to pursue the truth.

FIFA AND FOOTBALL

The Fédération Internationale de Football Association (FIFA) was founded in Paris, France, in 1904. The organization's goal was to create standardized rules for the game and to host international competitions. Until 1909, only European soccer associations were FIFA members.

When it started, FIFA had seven member countries—all European. Today, the organization includes over 200 soccer associations, or groups of soccer **clubs**, from all around the world. Every four years, it stages the World Cup, the largest sporting event in the world.

A DECADE OF DIGGING

For the next four years, Andrew reviewed the FIFA paperwork and gathered evidence to show that FIFA executives had mismanaged money, accepted bribes, and illegally sold World Cup tickets. He reviewed stacks of secret documents and emails that FIFA employees sent to him. And he interviewed hundreds of football insiders. Slowly, he pieced together his report on the crooked FIFA executives.

Like all investigative journalists, Andrew could not present his story to the public until he was 100 percent certain it was true. Every detail had to be checked, double-checked, and confirmed by multiple sources. To do this, Andrew practiced "slow, methodical journalism," taking the time he needed to be absolutely certain of his facts.

Andrew had a huge, international network of contacts. He used this network to help him research this story. He spoke to people he knew who connected him to other people who had information about FIFA. Some of the people he connected with gave him private e-mails that related to the FIFA story. Others provided him with secret financial information that proved FIFA executives took bribes or transferred money to their own bank accounts.

He interviewed many people in the football world, along with current and former politicians and past employees of companies that worked with FIFA.

Andrew also used the technique of ambushing the people he thought were involved in crimes. For example, he would wait for a certain person to come out of an office building.

Ambushing is a technique used by some investigative journalists to gather new information. In public places, they confront, or ambush, people who would not otherwise speak to them.

Then he'd run after that person, asking tough questions. Andrew received a lot of information based on the individual's reaction to his questions. As an experienced journalist, Andrew could tell when he had brought up a subject that FIFA did not want anyone to know about.

Naturally, many people didn't appreciate his pushy approach. Over the years, he was assaulted by FIFA executives he approached. One spit on him. Others hit him. They yelled at him, using foul language. Their lawyers sent him threatening letters. Not one of the FIFA executives Andrew approached ever agreed to be interviewed.

It wasn't just the people he investigated who treated Andrew badly, though. His fellow sports reporters wanted nothing to do with him or his story. They didn't want FIFA to think they were in on the investigation. Sports reporters have an unusual relationship with the teams they cover. They get free tickets (usually the best seats in the house) to local, national, and international sporting events. They meet players, hang out in locker rooms after games, and often receive gifts from the teams and their managers. "They like to be part of the show," wrote a SportsNet reporter in 2015.

These journalists report scores and play-by-play action on the field. They interview players and coaches. They track statistics and superstars. They *don't* cover scandals. If they did, they'd be banished from games and lose their on- and off-field privileges—just like Andrew did.

Andrew Jennings didn't care about any of that. Like most investigative journalists, all that mattered to him was exposing the truth. He never stopped digging.

"As other journalists were ball watching—reporting scorelines or writing player profiles—Jennings was digging into the dirty deals underpinning the world's most popular game."

Michael E. Miller, *Washington Post*, 2015

Through his research, he discovered that FIFA's criminal activity affected soccer associations around the world—in North and South America, Europe, Africa, and Asia. He discovered that FIFA executives knew there were problems within the organization, but nobody did anything about it. The people at the top made sure their actions were never questioned.

Finally, after four years of investigating, Andrew wrote his first book about his discoveries about FIFA. *FOUL! The Secret World of FIFA* was published in 2006. It focused on FIFA executives who had accepted bribes, abused power, and rigged voting to make sure certain countries won the right to host World Cup events.

Later that year, Andrew also helped produce a half-hour television segment on British TV about the FIFA executives who had accepted bribes.

The book and TV segment didn't draw much attention. Nor did a second TV episode a year later.

Still, Andrew kept investigating. Like many investigative journalism projects, this one kept expanding. For four more years, Andrew traveled the world, **networking**, observing, and talking to other journalists.

Even though sports reporters had distanced themselves from Andrew because of his FIFA research, some investigative journalists were eager to help him. Andrew had been banned from FIFA events, meaning he could no longer attend games, press conferences, or other events.

But other journalists could—and did. They gathered information, interviewed people, and videotaped activities, then passed it all to Andrew.

Andrew also continued to receive information from insiders. People with information now knew they could trust him to keep their names secret. They contacted him, offering new evidence against FIFA executives—bank records, e-mails, and other private paperwork.

Collaboration is often a key part of long-term, investigative projects. Sometimes other journalists have access to new sources or can help interpret information in new ways.

PROTECTING SOURCES

One of Andrew Jennings's biggest challenges in investigating the wrongdoing at FIFA was getting people to talk to him.

FIFA executives and officials refused to be interviewed. That meant Andrew had to find other sources of information. Sources might be written documents, audio recordings, or videos. They can be such things as private papers, books, maps, and social media posts. Sources can also be people.

During his 13-year investigation, Andrew interviewed hundreds of people—FIFA employees, football fans, game officials, and other journalists.

However, because FIFA executives wanted this story kept quiet, people put themselves at risk if they chose to speak to Andrew. They might have lost their jobs, been kicked out of the sport, or otherwise been treated badly by FIFA.

Protecting sources is something Andrew took very seriously. He needed information, but he also respected that people were afraid to speak up. "It took a long time building those sources and making them feel safe that I would never, ever reveal their identities," he said.

After people agreed to speak with Andrew, he still had to confirm that the information they provided was true. Investigative journalists must always double-check their information and confirm it with a variety of sources, before publishing it.

EXPOSING CRIMES

The new information Andrew received from sources and fellow journalists showed him that the crimes in international football weren't limited to FIFA executives. He found evidence that proved the heads of the South American, African, and Brazilian football associations had accepted bribes in exchange for voting for certain countries to host World Cup events.

He also found out that the vice-president of FIFA, a man from Trinidad named Jack Warner, had illegally sold tickets to 2006 World Cup events. Jack had purchased tickets, then re-sold them to fans at excessive prices. He made more than a million dollars from these sales. In 2010, Andrew helped produce "FIFA's Dirty Secrets," another, longer, TV segment about FIFA. In it, he revealed the new information he'd uncovered—the crimes by the African and South American football executives and Jack Warner's illegal ticket sales. Like the first TV show, this one didn't draw a huge public audience. By this time, though, Andrew was no longer completely alone in his efforts to expose wrongdoing at FIFA. "I had colleagues in other countries, particularly in Switzerland and Brazil, and we shared information, we shared documents," he said. "We were committed to the story."

By this time, too, Andrew's work—his books and TV segments—had caught the attention of a powerful law enforcement agency. A one-time British **secret service** agent had read Andrew's book, *Foul: The Secret World of FIFA*.

*A country may **bid** to host the World Cup for many reasons. Hosting the tournament can earn a country money and create jobs. It can also improve a country's international reputation.*

*Jack Warner **allegedly** accepted a $10 million bribe to vote for South Africa to host the World Cup in 2010.*

He brought the story to the attention of the American Federal Bureau of Investigation (FBI). In 2009, the former British agent set up a meeting between Andrew and the FBI.

The FBI had already launched an investigation into the American connections to the FIFA scandal. The organization wanted Andrew's help. For the next six years, Andrew helped the FBI with its criminal investigation, while he continued with his own journalistic investigation.

In 2014, Andrew released his second book on the FIFA scandal. In this one, entitled *Omertà*, he reported that FIFA executives had run an organized crime operation for decades. They'd accepted bribes, sold event tickets illegally, given themselves tens of millions of dollars in bonuses, and rigged voting to determine which countries hosted World Cup events. Andrew had enough evidence to prove that many executives were involved in organized crime—and the FBI agreed.

In May 2015, police in Switzerland and the United States arrested 14 FIFA executives. They were charged with bribery, **fraud**, and other offenses related to organized crime. "The world was stunned," wrote *The Washington Post*.

Suddenly, the story Andrew Jennings had been investigating for the previous 13 years made headlines around the world. International media outlets that had ignored the story quickly produced newspaper, radio, television, and online reports about the wrongdoing at FIFA. "It's taken the press a long time to catch up," said Andrew soon after the arrests.

The executives were arrested at the hotel Baur au Lac (below) in Zurich, Switzerland's largest city.

CHANGE-MAKING JOURNALISM

It may have taken other journalists a long time to catch up with Andrew's investigative work, but after the arrests, many were quick to praise him for his "dogged obsession," his "painstaking work," and his feverish devotion, dedication, and passion.

To Andrew, these things are just part of the job for an investigative journalist. "Our job is to discover the documents, amass the evidence and get the sources," he said. "That is hard work, but I have not found it hard to keep going. Your heart lifts every other day as a new piece of evidence comes along."

The evidence, which Andrew started gathering in 2002, ultimately led to the downfall of dozens of people. In total, 42 individuals and 3 companies were charged with 92 separate crimes and 15 organized crime schemes. Crimes included such things as fraud, bribery, racketeering, or committing crimes to make money, money laundering, or hiding money that was gained illegally, **forgery**, and not paying **taxes**. Trials started in 2017 and are expected to last five years.

Meanwhile, FIFA has conducted an internal investigation and made a number of policy changes to ensure such corruption never happens again. Dozens of football officials around the world—including Sepp Blatter—have resigned or been forced out of FIFA.

The organization has not yet recovered from the scandal.
A recent survey of 25,000 football fans showed that 98 percent said they "remain concerned about corruption at FIFA."

Andrew Jennings, now in his mid-70s, continues to work as an independent investigative journalist.

> For years [Andrew Jennings] was saying things that sounded quite outrageous, that people could not accept, people didn't want to hear. In fact, 15 years after investigating FIFA, everything he said is proven to be true.

Michael Gavshon, producer of *60 Minutes* news magazine

In September 2015, four months after the police raids on FIFA, Andrew Jennings published his third book about FIFA. In *The Dirty Game*, he documented how he uncovered the scandal. Two months later, his investigation was the focus of an hour-long documentary entitled, *FIFA, Sepp Blatter and Me*.

In recent years, Andrew has earned a number of awards for his work. Some are directly related to his FIFA investigation. Others are honors that celebrate his commitment to exposing wrongdoing in international sports.

Andrew (right) received the Play the Game Award in 2011. It honors people who have strengthened ethics in sports through their professional or volunteer work.

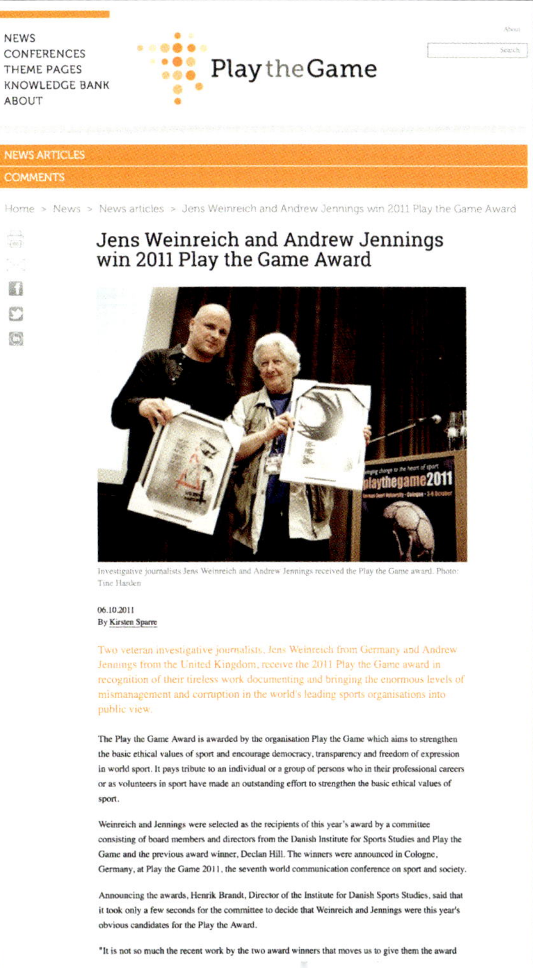

NEWS
CONFERENCES
THEME PAGES
KNOWLEDGE BANK
ABOUT

Play the Game

About

Search

NEWS ARTICLES

COMMENTS

Home > News > News articles > Jens Weinreich and Andrew Jennings win 2011 Play the Game Award

Jens Weinreich and Andrew Jennings win 2011 Play the Game Award

Investigative journalists Jens Weinreich and Andrew Jennings received the Play the Game award. Photo: Tine Harden

06.10.2011
By Kirsten Sparre

Two veteran investigative journalists, Jens Weinreich from Germany and Andrew Jennings from the United Kingdom, receive the 2011 Play the Game award in recognition of their tireless work documenting and bringing the enormous levels of mismanagement and corruption in the world's leading sports organisations into public view.

The Play the Game Award is awarded by the organisation Play the Game which aims to strengthen the basic ethical values of sport and encourage democracy, transparency and freedom of expression in world sport. It pays tribute to an individual or a group of persons who in their professional careers or as volunteers in sport have made an outstanding effort to strengthen the basic ethical values of sport.

Weinreich and Jennings were selected as the recipients of this year's award by a committee consisting of board members and directors from the Danish Institute for Sports Studies and Play the Game and the previous award winner, Declan Hill. The winners were announced in Cologne, Germany, at Play the Game 2011, the seventh world communication conference on sport and society.

Announcing the awards, Henrik Brandt, Director of the Institute for Danish Sports Studies, said that it took only a few seconds for the committee to decide that Weinreich and Jennings were this year's obvious candidates for the Play the Award.

"It is not so much the recent work by the two award winners that moves us to give them the award

"PUNCHED OUT"

WHO	Hockey player Derek Boogaard
WHAT	Suffered brain injury and drug abuse, which led to an early death
WHEN	2011
WHERE	Minneapolis, Minnesota
WHY	The culture of fighting in the National Hockey League

Sports and athletics are usually fun, entertaining, and healthy pursuits. You might think there's no reason for journalists to investigate such positive activities. Professional sports, however, often involve great amounts of money and glory. Sometimes, the pursuit of those things leads athletes, coaches, and others in the sporting world to behave in unethical ways.

Reporters around the world cover sports scandals and other wrongdoing to try to keep the games clean and safe. Sometimes, it's not the individuals involved in a sport who are the problem. Sometimes, it's the sport itself—the culture of the sport, the fans' expectations, or the accepted behavior of athletes—that are worth investigating. This was the case for a *New York Times* reporter in 2011.

In May of that year, National Hockey League (NHL) player Derek Boogaard died suddenly. He was only 28 years old. Derek's death caught the attention of an editor at the *The New York Times* for several reasons. Derek was young; he was a small-town Canadian boy living his dream of playing in the big leagues; and he died after **overdosing** on alcohol and prescription painkillers.

Derek Boogaard was born in Saskatchewan, Canada. He began playing hockey at a young age.

> Enforcers are seen as **working-class** superheroes [...] willing to do the sport's most dangerous work to protect others. And they are underdogs, men who otherwise might have no business in the game.
>
> **John Branch, *The New York Times*, 2011**

The editor wondered how such a successful athlete could die so young and so tragically. He asked sports reporter John Branch to look into it. At first, John wasn't interested. It wasn't his kind of reporting. He liked to tell short, fast-paced stories that he could research and write in a day or two. The editor insisted, though, so John agreed to do some research.

Within two weeks, John realized that there was more to the story than an overdose death of a famous athlete. He knew that this was a "fascinating" story that needed to be told. Like most investigative journalists, John was driven by curiosity, a commitment to finding the truth, and the desire to raise awareness of an important issue.

He spent the next six months piecing together a report on Derek's life and death. What he discovered was a hockey culture that celebrated violence and cared little about the suffering this violence caused players like Derek. He found that Derek was one of many hockey players who had suffered extreme brain damage, caused by repeated hits to the head. He found that the culture of violence in North American hockey leagues had contributed to Derek's death.

THE LIFE OF A HOCKEY PLAYER

Derek Boogaard had always loved to play hockey, but he was too big and slow to zip around the ice. At 6 feet 7 inches (2 m) and more than 265 pounds (120 kg), he was perfect for another role on the rink. He became an enforcer, a player whose job was to fight players on opposing teams.

After playing—and beating up other enforcers—in junior and minor hockey leagues, Derek caught the attention of National Hockey League (NHL) **scouts**. In 2005, he joined the Minnesota Wild, and for the next five years, fought his way to hockey superstardom. Other players feared Derek, but his fans and teammates loved what he did.

North American junior and **minor leagues** and the NHL are the only hockey leagues in the world that **tolerate** fighting. Officially, it's against the rules in these leagues, but it has long been part of the game's culture. Referees allow it, sports reporters celebrate it, and fans cheer when two players start belting each other on the ice. Sports networks replay the fights over and over again. There are websites devoted to showing hockey fights. Others rank players on their fighting skills and keep scores—the number of fights a player wins, loses, or ties. All of this puts pressure on enforcers like Derek to keep fighting, no matter how badly they get hurt.

In other sports, and other countries' hockey leagues, players who fight are kicked out of the game. In NHL hockey, they get just a five-minute penalty. Then they're back on the ice. Almost half of all NHL games stop mid-game because fights break out. "It's part of the game," said Matt Sommerfeld, a former minor league enforcer.

Unfortunately for the fighters, this part of the game means a lot of pain. They don't wear gloves during on-ice brawls, so their hands get cut, torn, and broken.

As a teen, Derek was coached to fight to improve his chances of playing hockey professionally. The strategy worked, and he became a Minnesota Wild star known as "the Boogeyman."

They don't wear helmets while they fight, so they get broken noses, teeth, and jaws. They also receive blows to the head that can lead to **concussions** and other brain damage.

By early 2009, Derek had suffered so many hits to his head that his behavior, on and off the ice, began to change. He got headaches. His memory failed. He became disoriented and blacked out. Sometimes, he forgot where he was.

To cope with the pain from the regular violence his body and mind endured, Derek drank a lot of alcohol and took prescription painkillers and sleeping pills. Most hockey enforcers take painkillers to dull the daily ache of their battered bodies. Some, including Derek, become addicted to those painkillers.

Because of his addiction, Derek entered a **rehabilitation** program in spring 2009. Eighteen months later, the Minnesota Wild traded him to the New York Rangers.

After playing just 21 games for New York, Derek was hurt so badly in an on-ice fight that he had to take some time away from the game he loved.

As he recovered from his physical injuries, he entered rehab for a second time. On May 12, 2011, medical staff allowed Derek to leave the facility for a few days. His brother was in charge of Derek's care during this break. Within hours of leaving the rehab center, Derek began drinking alcohol and taking pills. He consumed such great quantities of both that, by the next morning, he was dead.

Scientists at Boston University immediately asked Derek's parents to donate their son's brain for medical research. They agreed.

New York Times reporter John Branch began his research into Derek Boogaard's life and death about two weeks later.

Head injuries such as skull fractures (below) are common in hockey players.

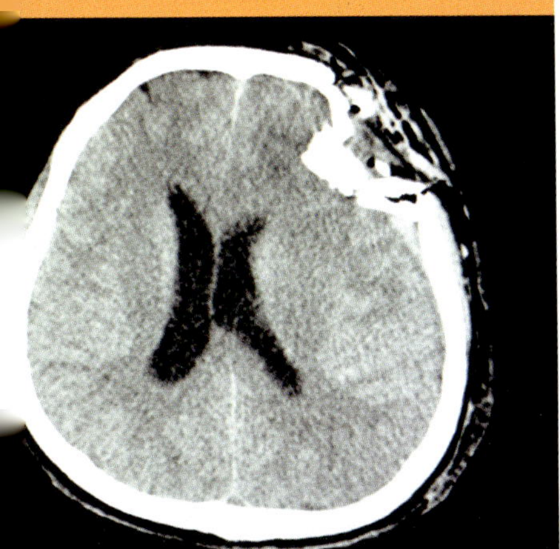

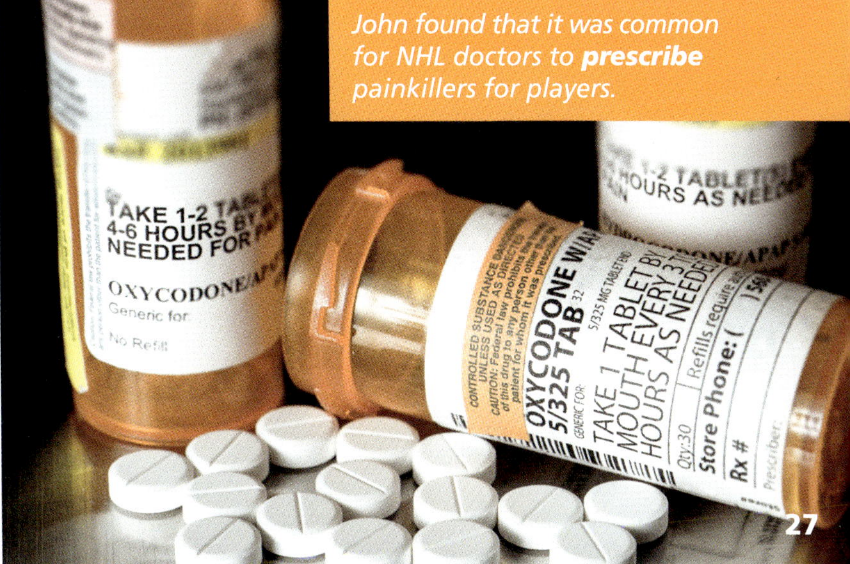

John found that it was common for NHL doctors to ***prescribe*** *painkillers for players.*

THE INVESTIGATION BEGINS

Investigative journalists never rely on a single person or piece of information. Collecting accurate details from a variety of sources takes time, and is one of the reasons a journalistic investigation can take months or even years to complete.

During the following six months, John interviewed dozens of people who had known Derek. He talked to coaches, teammates, childhood friends, former girlfriends, hockey scouts, and other NHL enforcers. The story would not have been possible, though, without Derek's parents.

Convincing them to speak publicly about their son was one of John's biggest challenges. At first, Derek's parents were "suspicious" about how the newspaper would portray Derek. When John explained he would be fair and accurate in his reporting—and that he was going to tell the story with them or without them—they agreed to participate.

Some sources may wish to speak "off-the-record." This usually means that they provide the journalist with information that could help with their investigation, but they do not want their words included in the journalist's story. Other times, sources may allow a journalist to publish their words, but wish to remain unnamed.

Journalists commonly use interviews as a way of gathering information from different perspectives.

It is important for journalists to respect the privacy of their sources.

Investigative journalists, like all reporters, follow codes of ethics that guide their behavior. These codes include such things as reporting the truth, getting all sides of a story, and not twisting people's words or taking them out of **context**.

Over the next few months, John interviewed members of the Boogaard family a number of times about a variety of different topics. They gave John private papers, videos of Derek on and off the ice, scrapbooks, newspaper clippings, photographs, and medical records.

They also gave him Derek's personal journal, so he could add Derek's voice to the story. The journal entries allowed John to include details that nobody but Derek would have known. They also helped John understand Derek better, and pass on that understanding to his readers.

John used information from all these resources to pull together his story. He read through every document, watched every video, and kept track of the masses of information he gathered from all those different sources.

DIFFERENT PERSPECTIVES

Investigative journalism stories can be told in a variety of different media. Media is the plural form of the word medium. A medium is a method of mass communication, a way to deliver information to a wide variety of people.

Some stories are presented as newspaper or online text articles with photographs. Others are told on radio through sound. Television and other online media outlets use video images to present their stories. The Internet uses digital technology.

Because most investigative journalism projects end up online these days, many media outlets take advantage of the technology and blend many of the storytelling types. Such multimedia presentations can include photos, as well as video, audio, and written components. Maps, charts, infographics, and interactive visual elements are also common.

Different audiences process information in different ways, so providing a variety of storytelling techniques means journalists reach broader audiences.

NEW ANGLES

The more John researched, the more angles he discovered to his story—including the connection between brain damage and on-ice fighting, how easy it is for players to access prescription drugs, and the emotional pressure hockey enforcers suffer.

This can often happen—once journalists start digging, they find other unexpected twists and turns worth covering. Sometimes, this leads a reporter in a completely different direction than the one in which he or she started.

To accommodate all the new information John discovered during his research, his final project changed from being a single story by a single reporter to being a series of stories and a major multimedia project. At that point, he began working with photographers, videographers, video editors, and other technical experts to tell the story in a variety of different media formats.

While John was investigating Derek's life for his news stories, Derek's father—a police officer—was conducting his own investigation into his son's death. Len Boogaard called every contact in Derek's phone.

Derek's career in the NHL depended on his fighting. In his 277 NHL game appearances, he scored just three goals. He spent 1,411 minutes on ice and 589 minutes in the penalty box.

He analyzed medical reports and his son's history with prescription drugs. He shared everything he learned with John.

One shocking thing Len shared with John was that, in one three-month period in the 2008–2009 hockey season, eight different NHL doctors prescribed 11 different painkiller prescriptions to Derek.

"Most NHL teams have about 10 doctors—specialists and dentists with practices of their own," wrote John. "[Derek] had learned that there was no system to track who was prescribing what."

As he needed more and more pills to feed his addiction, Derek visited more and more doctors to get different prescriptions.

John added this information to his story. Investigative journalists must report on all sides of the story, but the perspective of the NHL teams involved, the Minnesota Wild and the New York Rangers, and the team doctors are missing from this one. That's because they refused requests to speak with Len Boogaard. They also refused to answer a list of questions about their medical treatment of Derek. The details that led to Derek becoming addicted to huge amounts of painkillers may never be fully known.

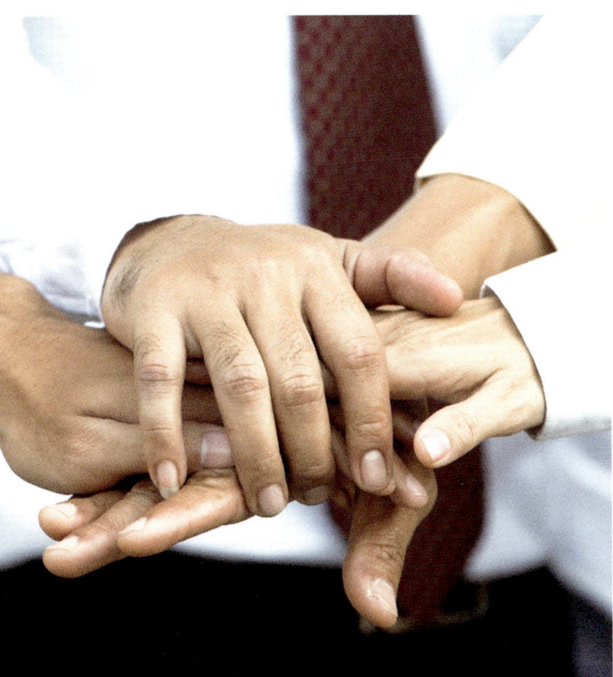

As John's story progressed, he collaborated with other journalism professionals to add details and engaging elements, such as photos, to his project.

With father Len's help, John added new details in the story such as Derek being overprescribed painkillers. These help paint a picture of how Derek was encouraged to keep fighting.

CHANGE-MAKING JOURNALISM

In October 2011, Derek Boogaard's parents got the results of the medical research on their son's brain. The research revealed that Derek had chronic traumatic encephalopathy (CTE). This is brain damage caused by repeated blows to the head. Derek's parents chose to share this information with John, so that he could share it with the public. Immediately, John's investigation took off in a new direction—and like most journalists, he went after it.

John had never written about CTE, so he had a lot to learn. Journalists often have to research new subjects before they can write their reports. They have to understand the topic, so they can explain it to the public. Fortunately, another reporter at *The New York Times*, Alan Schwartz, was a CTE expert. He'd written more than 100 articles about brain injury in the National Football League. John talked to Alan and read his articles and notes about CTE to learn about the disease.He also interviewed a variety of medical experts on the subject of CTE, and tried to talk to NHL doctors and executives about it. None of the hockey people would talk to him. Nor would they talk to Derek's parents.

One of the directors of the Boston Medical Center said she'd never seen such an advanced degree of brain damage in someone as young as Derek. It likely contributed to his death, but it was impossible to tell whether Derek's addiction had led to CTE or if CTE had led to his addiction.

In early December 2011, seven months after Derek Boogaard's death, *The New York Times* published John Branch's three-part series on the hockey player's life and death. It also presented a half-hour documentary on its website, entitled *Punched Out: The Death of Derek Boogaard.*

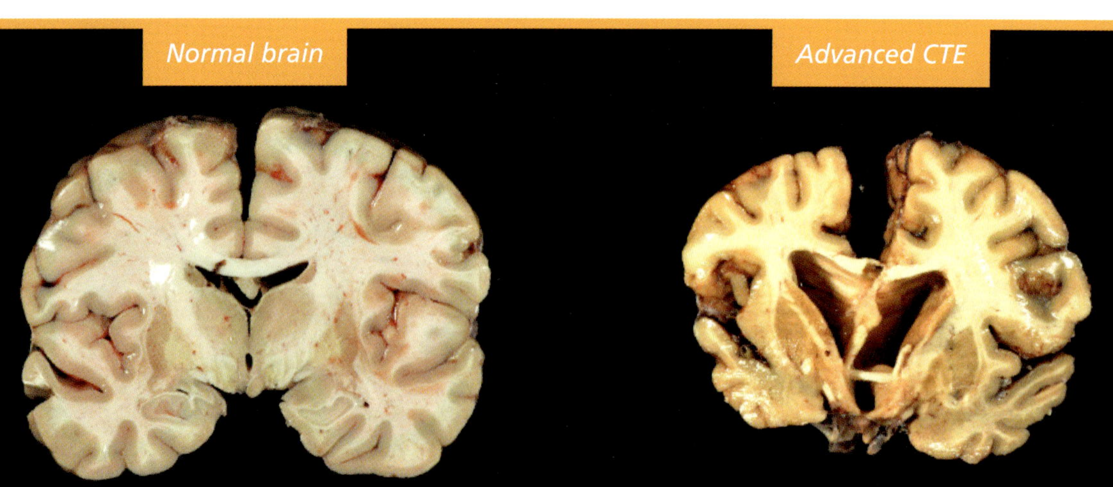

When they received the results of Derek's brain analysis, the Boogaards were shocked at the severe damage the organ showed.

John's series won two national journalism awards and was nominated for a Pulitzer Prize, the most prestigious award for American journalists. Three years later, John wrote a book based on his investigation, *Boy on Ice: The Life and Death of Derek Boogaard*.

Today, John remains a sports reporter for *The New York Times*. While his stories about Derek Boogaard led to little change in the NHL, they raised awareness of the dangers of head injuries in the league. They also stirred up the ongoing debate about fighting in the NHL.

Since the stories ran, junior and minor leagues have increased the penalties for fighting during games. In some circumstances, players who fight are kicked off the ice for the rest of the game. Mostly, they get a 10-minute visit to the penalty box. The hope is that increased penalties will deter players from fighting.

After Derek Boogaard's death, his brother was charged with distributing drugs because he admitted he gave Derek a painkiller the night he died. That charge was dropped, but he pleaded guilty to tampering with evidence. He admitted he had flushed Derek's pills down the toilet before police arrived at the death scene.

Derek's parents sued the NHL for the wrongful death of their son. That case was dismissed in 2018. Meanwhile, a group of about 300 former NHL players is in the midst of a lawsuit against the NHL over the way it deals with concussion and CTE in its players. The players say they believe the league knew, or should have known, there was a link between repeated head injuries and long-term brain damage—and should have done more to protect the athletes.

BRAIN DAMAGE

After Derek Boogaard died, researchers analyzed his brain and discovered that he suffered from chronic traumatic encephalopathy (CTE). This is a type of brain damage that leads to memory loss, confusion, headaches, addiction, aggressive behavior, depression, and other personality changes.

It is caused by repeated hits to the head—but not necessarily hard hits to the head. "You don't have to have concussions to end up with this disease," said *New York Times* reporter John Branch.

The damage done by a series of small blows can eventually add up to CTE. The disease can only be detected after a person dies and his or her brain is analyzed.

Derek was the fourth deceased NHL player to be diagnosed with CTE in four years. Still, the league doesn't believe there's a connection between hockey and CTE.

A decade ago, the National Football League (NFL) didn't believe there was a connection between football and CTE. Since then, scientists have found the disease in 99 percent of deceased NFL players whose brains were donated for research.

"OUT OF BALANCE"

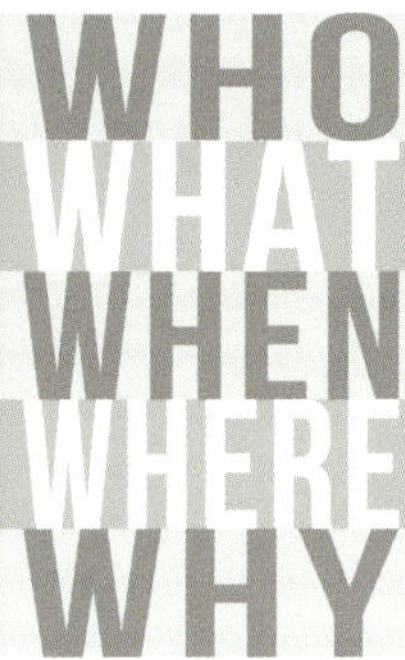

Gymnasts

Abused by team doctors and coaches

For decades

All over the United States

A USA Gymnastics policy to *not* report accusations of abuse

Often, investigative journalists get tips that lead to a story, or change the direction of a project in progress. This was the situation for *Indianapolis Star (IndyStar)* reporter Marisa Kwiatkowski. In March 2016, she was investigating unreported child abuse in schools and daycares. During her research, someone she met gave her a tip about child abuse in national-level gymnastics.

The source suggested Marisa look into a lawsuit a gymnast in Georgia had filed against her coach. The girl had also filed a lawsuit against the national gymnastics association, USA Gymnastics (USAG), for not protecting her from abuse.

Marisa knew this could be a big story. "I flew to Georgia later that day, and picked up almost 1,000 pages of court records," she said. As soon as she and her *IndyStar* colleagues—Tim Evans and Mark Alesia— began reading the legal papers, they knew they had to tell this story. They began working on it right away.

Court records and other legal documents are good sources for investigative journalists. They contain factual information, witness statements, and timelines of events and criminal activities. The investigative journalist's job is to gather evidence for a story and prove that it's true. Legal documents offer such proof.

For four-and-a-half months, the three reporters and a team of photographers and videographers traveled the country interviewing gymnasts, coaches, gym owners, and representatives of organizations that work to protect children. They spoke to the mother of the girl who had filed the Georgia lawsuit and other victims and their families. They interviewed lawyers and detectives to understand the laws about reporting child abuse.

They learned that the gymnast in Georgia wasn't the only athlete to have been abused by her coach, and her coach wasn't the only coach who had abused young gymnasts.

According to USAG, more than 200,000 gymnasts are part of the organization.

> It's not often that a story has such a broad and **sustained** impact. Our newsroom truly **rallied** around the coverage. The time and expense of this investigation was not small, but we felt it paled in comparison to the impact of the story.

Jeff Taylor, USA Today Network (owner of *IndyStar*), 2018

While Aly Raisman (below) and Team USA competed for Olympic gold in Rio de Janeiro in August 2016, Marisa, Tim, and Mark were investigating and exposing USAG's wrongdoing.

REPORTING THE TRUTH

To verify that the information they received was true, the reporters filed **Freedom of Information (FOI)** requests for public records in 10 different states. Through this process, they received and reviewed thousands of pages of court records, police reports, and other federal and state documents. They also went to court to ask a judge to grant access to legal documents sealed from public view.

Because journalists must report all points of view in a story, the *IndyStar* reporters also requested interviews with current and former executives from USAG. They wanted to hear their sides of the story. The executives declined to be interviewed, as did gymnastics coaches who'd already been found guilty of abusing young athletes.

In August 2016, Marisa and her colleagues published their first collection of stories on the *IndyStar* website. The package, titled "Out of Balance," consisted of 10 stories and videos, along with photos, timelines, and links to documents. It documented the crimes of four Olympic-level gymnastics coaches who had abused young athletes. Three of the four were in jail. The fourth had killed himself in prison.

Some of the coaches' abuse had gone on for decades—and USAG had done nothing to stop it. In fact, as the reporters revealed, USAG had a policy not to report accusations of abuse to police, unless the complaints came directly from athletes or their parents. In most cases, the abused athletes were preteen or teenaged girls who were afraid to speak up.

USAG had ignored complaints from gym owners, other athletes, and people who had witnessed or overheard conversations about abuse. Rather than reporting these complaints to police—as the law required—USAG filed them in a desk drawer in its Indianapolis head office.

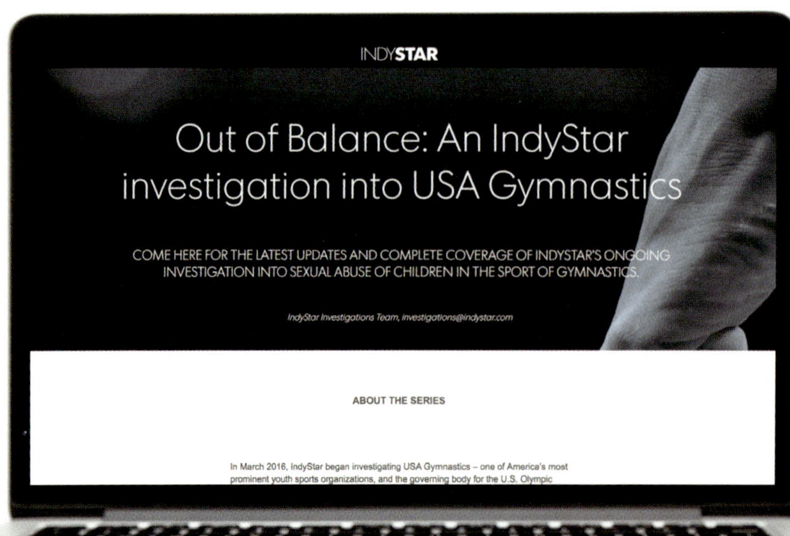

"Out of Balance" revealed that USA Gymnastics was purposely hiding reports that coaches were abusing athletes—allowing the abuse to continue for many years.

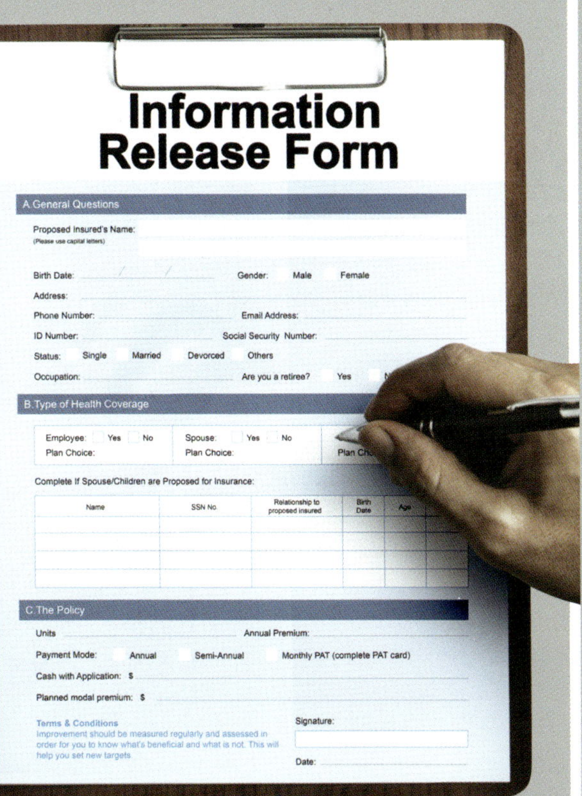

In some cases, FOI requests are denied to protect such things as personal information and data that could harm a country's security.

BREAKING THE SILENCE

Investigative journalists often need information that isn't available to the public.

Sometimes, it's paperwork the government wants to keep secret. In that case, reporters can submit Freedom of Information (FOI) requests to get the papers. Most countries have FOI laws to prevent governments from keeping secrets from their citizens. Any citizen, including a journalist, can request access to government documents under these laws.

Sometimes, documents aren't available to the public for legal reasons. In those situations, the reporters must submit a request to a judge to make the documents available. The *IndyStar* reporters had to go through this process.

Through their research into gymnastics abuse, they had learned that USA Gymnastics (USAG) had received complaints about 54 different gymnastics coaches. The coaches' names and details of the complaints weren't available to the public because the information was part of a lawsuit filed by a young gymnast in Georgia. In abuse cases, details are often kept secret to protect the people involved.

In June 2016, the *IndyStar* asked a judge to open the USAG files. "Those records contain important information related to the safety of thousands of young gymnasts who train under USA Gymnastics coaches," wrote reporter Tim Evans.

USAG opposed the request, saying releasing the information would harm coaches and the organization.

The judge sided with the newspaper and ordered USAG to release the documents. The paperwork revealed the names and histories of the accused coaches, many of whom were still working with children.

THE STORY GROWS

The day the first set of gymnastics stories ran, a former gymnast living in Louisville, Kentucky, emailed the *IndyStar*. "I recently read the article titled 'Out of Balance' published by the *IndyStar*," wrote Rachael Denhollander. "My experience may not be relevant to your investigation, but I am emailing to report an incident that may be. I was not **molested** by my coach, but I was molested by Dr. Larry Nassar, the team doctor for USAG."

Rachael later said she sent the e-mail because, after reading "Out of Balance," she thought the reporters would listen to her story. Until then, she'd never spoken up because she thought nobody would believe her.

Investigative journalists often receive calls from other victims, or other people involved, after their stories are published. Seeing a fair, thorough, well-researched report sometimes gives people the courage to share their own stories.

Not only did Marisa, Tim, and Mark believe Rachael, but they immediately started another investigation—this time into Dr. Nassar.

They divided the work to investigate this new lead. Each reporter interviewed different sources and followed different lines of research. Mark interviewed Rachael, Marisa interviewed another woman who had come forward with her story, and Mark focused on Nassar's history as a physician.

*Along with many other women, Rachael bravely read an **impact statement** in court describing how Nassar's abuse affected her.*

While they worked on this new story, they wrote and published another eight stories related to the first one—including other gymnasts' stories of abuse, government reaction to the first set of stories, and features on how to spot and prevent child abuse.

In September 2016, they published the story of how Dr. Nassar had abused Rachael and another gymnast. Because journalists must cover all points of view in a story, one of the reporters also interviewed the doctor. He denied any wrongdoing. Nine days later, he was fired from his job at Michigan State University, and by the end of the month, 16 women—including Rachael—had filed criminal complaints against him.

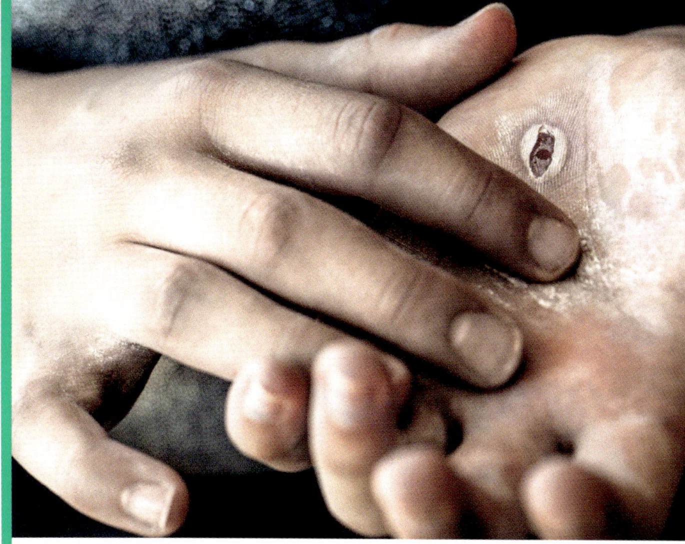

THE SPORTING LIFE

Most of the world's top-level gymnasts dedicate their early lives to the sport. They start training as young children and reach the peak of their careers in their teens and early-20s.

They train daily, often spending 30 to 40 hours a week in the gym. This leaves little time for a social life. They risk injury to their still-growing bodies—such as broken bones, sprained joints, torn muscles, and bleeding hands.

In addition, the sport is highly competitive. Gymnasts who want to perform at international levels have to work harder than their competitors. They are constantly judged.

One wrong move might mean the difference between making the team and staying at home. For this reason, young gymnasts are often eager to please their coaches and other gymnastics officials.

Unfortunately, their need to please can make gymnasts targets for abuse by people in positions of authority, such as coaches or doctors. Young gymnasts may not speak up about abuse because they fear being kicked off the team.

CHANGE-MAKING JOURNALISM

For the three *IndyStar* journalists, the story of abuse within USA Gymnastics didn't end with Dr. Nassar. Every story they published led to another. "Once our first story ran about Nassar, almost daily, more women were coming forward" with reports of abuse against Dr. Nassar and other USAG coaches, said reporter Mark Alesia.

In a 17-month period, the journalists wrote more than three dozen stories documenting widespread abuse within the gymnastics world. Their research revealed that almost 370 gymnasts had made abuse claims against coaches and others over a 20-year period—but USAG had not followed up on the complaints.

Like many investigative journalism projects, "Out of Balance" was too big and complicated for a single person—or, in this case, three reporters—to handle. In total, nine reporters and editors, along with photographers and videographers, participated in the project.

IndyStar's "Out of Balance" series earned a number of state and national journalism awards. More importantly, said the reporters, it changed lives and led to major changes in the gymnastics world.

Dr. Larry Nassar was arrested in November 2016. By the time he went to court, more than 150 people had filed charges against him. For more than a year, he was in and out of court on various charges. He pleaded guilty to many of them and, in January 2018, was sentenced to up to 175 years in prison for his crimes against young people.

Ultimately, more than 250 women accused Nassar of abusing them.

"The hardest part [for us] was getting people to trust us to tell deeply **intimate** stories at a time when it was quite possible people weren't going to believe them. We were fortunate to have gained the trust of some really brave women."

***IndyStar* reporter Tim Evans, 2018**

In March 2017, the president and many executives at USAG resigned. In June 2017, an independent review reported that USAG had not done enough to make sure children were protected from abuse. It recommended a complete change of the organization. Days later, the board of directors of USAG wrote a **formal** apology to its members and athletes. They vowed to make the changes recommended in the report, which would make sure the organization better protected its athletes.

In January 2018, the United States Olympic Committee (USOC) ordered every member of that board of directors to resign. The USOC, which oversees national governing bodies for amateur sports, said if the directors didn't resign, it would shut down the gymnastics organization.

A month later, the U.S. government passed a law requiring all amateur sports organizations to report all claims of abuse.

Meanwhile, a number of gymnasts have filed lawsuits against a number of coaches and USA Gymnastics.

For the three reporters who initiated the gymnastics investigation, all of these changes are satisfying—but they say their work on this project is not done. Marisa Kwiatkowski said she and her *IndyStar* colleagues will continue their investigation into USAG, "in addition to other things we're working on."

When they're not investigating gymnastics, Marisa, Tim, and Mark report on social, legal, business, and sports issues for *IndyStar*.

These five gymnasts (from left, Kyla Ross , Jordyn Wieber, Aly Raisman, Gabby Douglas, and McKayla Maroney) were stars of the 2012 Olympics in London, England. Known as the "Fierce Five," they won gold for Team USA. All five have accused Nassar of abusing them.

CONCLUSION

The *IndyStar*'s in-depth coverage of the USA Gymnastics abuse scandal earned praise from journalists across the country. It was also applauded by the lawyer who led the court case against Larry Nassar. "We as a society need investigative journalists more than ever," said Michigan Assistant **Attorney General** Angela Povilaitis, who was one of the **prosecutors** in the Larry Nassar case.

This is why investigative reporters do what they do. They see wrongs that need to be righted. They see people mistreated. They see powerful people getting away with bad behavior, abusing authority, or committing crimes. Investigative journalists seek to report on such wrongdoing. They work hard to find and tell the truth. Their stories raise public awareness, hold powerful people responsible for their actions, and often lead to change.

In today's society, we are bombarded with information from a variety of sources. Newspapers and other media outlets are often viewed as old-fashioned. Social media has taken over as a major source of information. Many people don't have time to research what they hear and read, though, so they often blindly believe.

> I got into this business to give a voice to those who may not have one, and to expose wrongdoing and hopefully, at the end of the day, to improve the lives of the people we serve.

Marisa Kwiatkowski, 2018

Reading investigative journalism stories is one way we can learn about issues in all parts of society. The stories can be a starting point for people to push for positive change.

Unfortunately, much of the information presented doesn't tell the full story—or worse, it's presented by people who want to **mislead** the public.

That's why investigative journalism is so important these days. The reporters who tackle investigative projects take the time to do the research and to check (and double-check) the facts. They are willing to take personal and professional risks to tell the stories other people want to keep hidden.

Investigative journalism projects give voice to people who may not otherwise be heard. They allow citizens to make informed choices. And they reveal truths that the world needs to know.

BIBLIOGRAPHY

CHAPTER 1

"Investigative Journalism." UNESCO. https://bit.ly/2Pc6ERP

MacDonald, Hugh. "Brick by filthy brick: Andrew Jennings's relentless quest to expose FIFA." *The Sunday Herald*, October 2, 2015. https://bit.ly/2odQyvn

Panja, Tariq. "FIFA Set to Make $6.1 Billion From World Cup." *The New York Times*, June 12, 2018. https://nyti.ms/2PHeDr2

CHAPTER 2

Brunt, Stephen. "How one reporter helped to bring down Blatter." SportsNet, June 25, 2015. https://sprtsnt.ca/2My5kvA

Conn, David. "Trust in FIFA has improved only slightly under Gianni Infantino, survey finds." *The Guardian*, March 2, 2017. https://bit.ly/2ojknLi

MacDonald, Hugh. "Brick by filthy brick: Andrew Jennings's relentless quest to expose FIFA." *The Sunday Herald*, 2015. https://bit.ly/2odQyvn

Miller, Michael E. "How a curmudgeonly old reporter exposed the FIFA scandal that toppled Sepp Blatter." *The Washington Post*, June 3, 2015. https://wapo.st/2BSL1Ei

The Mob Museum. "Interview with journalist Andrew Jennings, who exposed FIFA scandal, is first entry in online video archive." Mob Museum video vault, October 6, 2016. https://bit.ly/2Pc20Dd

United Nations Office on Drugs and Crime. "United Nations Convention Against Transnational Organized Crime and the Protocols Thereto." United Nations, 2004. https://bit.ly/1vHv97q

CHAPTER 3

Branch, John. "Derek Boogaard: A Boy Learns to Brawl." *The New York Times*, December 3, 2011. https://nyti.ms/2BSoEyS

Branch, John. "Derek Boogaard: A Brain 'Going Bad'." *The New York Times*, December 5, 2011. https://nyti.ms/2MxsYZg

Branch, John. "Derek Boogaard: Blood on the Ice." *The New York Times*, December 4, 2011. https://nyti.ms/1CS5YF7

Mez, Jesse, et al. "Clinicopathological Evaluation of Chronic Traumatic Encephalopathy in Players of American Football." The Journal of the American Medical Association, June 25, 2017. https://bit.ly/2s3J7fb

SportsLetter. "SL Interview: John Branch on Derek Boogaard and CTE in Hockey." LA 84 Foundation, November 6, 2014. https://bit.ly/2PK5rlZ

CHAPTER 4

Bahr, Sarah. "AMA: Marisa Kwiatkowski, Journalist." *Indianapolis Monthly*, April 2018. https://bit.ly/2LyaEd7

CNN staff. "Read prosecutor's statement at Larry Nassar sentencing." CNN, 2018. https://cnn.it/2wiOM0B

Evans, Tim. "IndyStar seeks to unseal abuse documents." *IndyStar*, August 4, 2016. https://indy.st/2AS0IQL

Hobson, Jeremy. "How The Indianapolis Star Broke The Larry Nassar Sexual Abuse Story." WBUR radio, January 26, 2018. https://wbur.fm/2LwOOGM

Manes, Nick. "Q&A: Marisa Kwiatkowski, Investigative Reporter at The Indianapolis Star." MiBiz, 2018. https://bit.ly/2PIfQys

USA Today Network Pressroom staff. "The *IndyStar* brings justice to Nassar victims." USA Today Network, January 26, 2018. https://usat.ly/2NpeCGI

LEARNING MORE

BOOKS

Doeden, Matt. *The World Cup: Soccer's Global Championship*, Millbrook Press, 2018.

Goldsmith, Connie. *Traumatic Brain Injury: From Concussion to Coma*, Twenty-First Century Books, 2014.

Ignotofsky, Rachel. *Women in Sports: 50 Fearless Athletes Who Played to Win.* Ten Speed Press, 2017.

WEBSITES

If you're interested in becoming a sports reporter, this web page, "How to: get into sports journalism," has some good information to get you started.
www.journalism.co.uk/skills/how-to-get-into-sports-journalism/s7/a552212

Time for Kids is filled with up-to-date, kid-friendly news and current events.
www.timeforkids.com/g56

This link on The Mob Museum website has videos about organized crime investigations. Two videos deal with Jennings's FIFA investigation. One is an interview with Andrew. The other is a short video summary of the FIFA scandal, "The 'Beautiful Game' Turns Ugly." Scroll down the page to find the videos.
https://themobmuseum.org/case-files/digital-experiences

LINKS TO ARTICLES IN THIS BOOK

Chapter 1–2

"FIFA's Dirty Secrets." *BBC Panorama*, 2010.
Part 1: **https://bit.ly/2wrV5Ox**
Part 2: **https://bit.ly/2wrULiN**

Oliver, James. "FIFA: Football's Shame?" *BBC Panorama*, 2014.
https://bit.ly/2MWO6rd

Chapter 3

Branch, John. "Derek Boogaard: A Boy Learns to Brawl." *The New York Times*, December 3, 2011. **https://nyti.ms/2BSoEyS**

Branch, John. "Derek Boogaard: A Brain 'Going Bad'." *The New York Times*, December 5, 2011.
https://nyti.ms/2MxsYZg

Branch, John. "Derek Boogaard: Blood on the Ice." *The New York Times*, December 4, 2011.
https://nyti.ms/1CS5YF7

Harris, Shayla. *Punched Out: The Death of Derek Boogaard. New York Times* Documentaries, 2014.
https://nyti.ms/2wpSZyN

Chapter 4

Kwiatkowski, Marisa, Mark Alesia, and Tim Evans. "Out of Balance: An IndyStar investigation into USA Gymnastics." *IndyStar*, 2016-2017.
https://bit.ly/2n9BPBH

GLOSSARY

administrative body The group of leaders who run a business or organization

allegedly Thought or said by some people, but not yet proven

ambushed Made a surprise attack

Attorney General The head legal officer who represents a country or state

bid To offer to do or buy something

bribes Money or other rewards offered in exchange for something

chaotic Confused, disordered, messy, out of control

clubs Organizations created to play games in a certain sport. A football club includes the team and other supporting members, such as coaches and managers.

concealed Hidden

concussions Head injuries that temporarily affect the brain's ability to function

contacts People who journalists connect with to share information

context The full discussion of a subject that allows a statement to be understood; taking something out of context means leaving out important information that would fully explain the situation

conventional Regular; follows commonly held beliefs or actions

copyright laws Laws that protect people's original work from being used or reproduced without their permission

corrupt Doing things that are dishonest or illegal to gain money or power

court The place where cases are argued and decided on by a judge

data analysts People who collect and analyze data, or information, and use it to solve a problem

distributed Sent out

editors People at a newspaper who choose stories to be featured and ensure they have no factual, spelling, or grammatical errors

ethics Ideas about right and wrong behavior

forgery Falsely creating or altering a written document

formal Official or important

fraud Deceiving someone to get money, power, or other personal gain

Freedom of Information (FOI) Laws that prevent a government from keeping secrets from its citizens

graphic designers Professionals who put together visuals, such as images, for any kind of media

Herr "Mister" in German

impact statement Testimony given in court by a victim or by a victim's family or friends. Impact statements detail the harm caused to the victim.

independent journalist A journalist who is self-employed, rather than working for a specific news outlet

International Olympic Committee The governing body responsible for organizing the modern Olympic Games

intimate Close, personal

legal Related to laws or court

minor leagues The leagues below the level of the major league in sports

mislead To give someone the wrong idea or information

molested Sexually assaulted, or abused by someone

multimedia Using a combination of forms in a single production or presentation

networking Interact with other people to exchange information and develop contacts

overdosing taking too much of a drug or medicine

prescribe The practice by medical professionals that advises and authorizes the use of medicine by a patient

press conference A meeting at which someone announces something or reveals information to a large number of journalists at the same time

proactive Taking action, rather than waiting for something to happen

prosecutors People, especially lawyers, who bring legal cases against others

public documents Documents available to the general public; includes many different kinds of legal, government, and business documents

rallied Supported, especially as a group

rehabilitation Treatment that helps restore someone to health

resigned Quit or left one's job

rigged Falsely determined an outcome so it benefited a certain person or group

scouts People who find new and talented athletes for sports teams

secret service A branch of government in some countries that focuses on national security and carries out criminal investigations

shunned Deliberately ignored or rejected

sources People, documents, videos, recordings, or other publications that provide information to a journalist

sustained Maintained, kept going

taxes Money paid to the government by citizens of a country and used to provide such things as education and health care

tolerate Allow, accept, or put up with something

United Nations An international organization made up of 193 countries that works to promote world peace and human rights

working-class People who work less-skilled jobs for wages or hourly pay; usually not college educated

INDEX

ABOUT THE AUTHOR

Diane Dakers has been a print and broadcast journalist since 1991. She specializes in culture, science, and business reporting. She has also written 24 nonfiction and three fiction books for youth.